Prince Lachlan.

For my little Prince and
his sisters the Princesses Royal

N.H.

For Dugal and others from the
peppery Stewart Clan

A.J.

Text copyright © 1989 by Nette Hilton
Illustrations copyright © 1989 by Ann James
First American Edition 1990 published by Orchard Books.
First published in Australia by Omnibus Books in association with Penguin
Books Australia.

Orchard Books, A division of Franklin Watts, Inc.
387 Park Avenue South, New York, NY 10016

Manufactured in the United States of America
Printed by General Offset Co., Inc.
Bound by Horowitz/Rae. Book design by Mina Greenstein
The text of this book is set in 18 pt. ITC Cheltenham Book.
The illustrations are pen and ink and watercolors, reproduced in full color.
10 9 8 7 6 5 4 3 2 1

Library of Congress Cataloging-in-Publication Data
Hilton, Nette. Prince Lachlan / written by Nette Hilton : illustrated by Ann James.
—1st American ed.   p.   cm. Summary: Noisy Prince Lachlan saves the day
when his noise frightens off the Great One who wants to steal the King's throne.
ISBN 0-531-05863-8.   ISBN 0-531-08463-9 (lib. bdg.)
[1. Noise—Fiction. 2. Kings, queens, rulers, etc.—Fiction.] I. James, Ann, ill.
II. Title. PZ7.H56775Pn 1990 [E]—dc20 89-22846 CIP AC

PRINCE LACHLAN

by Nette Hilton

illustrated by Ann James

ORCHARD BOOKS • NEW YORK

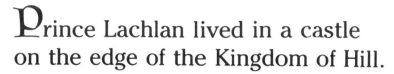

Prince Lachlan lived in a castle
on the edge of the Kingdom of Hill.

Crash went the drawbridge.
Slide went the rug.
Thud went the table.
Smash went the vase.

"Prince Lachlan is home," said the queen.
"I know," said the king.

Prince Lachlan's bedroom
was in the middle of the castle
on the edge of the Kingdom of Hill.
In it he kept all the things
he liked to play with.

Boom went the drum.
Blast went the trumpet.
Strum went the lute.
Woof went the dog.

"Prince Lachlan loves music," said the queen.
"I know," sighed the king.

Prince Lachlan had a courtyard
at the back of the castle
on the edge of the Kingdom of Hill.
In it he practiced all the games
he liked to play.

Zing went the slingshot.
"*Ouch*," said the gardener.
Crack went the flowerpot.
Woof, woof went the dog.

"Prince Lachlan loves games," said the queen.
"I know," said the king.

On the far side of the Kingdom of Hill
was the castle of the Great One.
It was filled with all the treasures
he had stolen.

Shine went the mirrors.
Glow went the gold.
Hush went the rugs on the wall.
But the Great One wanted more.

He wanted the throne that belonged to
King Ronald of the Kingdom of Hill.

"The Great One wants your throne," said the queen.
"I know," said the king.
"We'll see about that!" said Prince Lachlan.
And without another word
he set off to see the Great One.

Prince Lachlan took his ball to bounce
and his dog for company.

Boing, boing, boing went the ball
on the drawbridge to the Great One's castle.

Shatter went the window.
Tinkle went the glass.
Woof went the dog.
"Oops," said Prince Lachlan.

Robbers! thought the Great One.

Bash went the door.
"*Eeeek!*" said the maid.
Slop went the soup.
Meeowch! went the cat.
"Oh dear," said Prince Lachlan.

"Hide!" muttered the Great One.

Clatter went the armor.
Clunk went the sword.
Rrrrip went the tapestry.
Yip went the dog.
"This is fun!" said Prince Lachlan.

"I'm leaving!" said the Great One.
And without another word he ran away from the
Kingdom of Hill, and the thieves in his castle.

Prince Lachlan returned to his castle
on the edge of the Kingdom of Hill.
On the way he kicked a fat round rock
and whistled happily to his dog.

Whizz went the rock.
Crunch went the cornerstone.
Crumple went the corner of the castle of King Ronald.

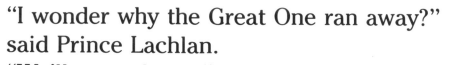

"I wonder why the Great One ran away?"
said Prince Lachlan.

"We'll never know," mused the queen.

"*I* know," said the king.